The Tortoise and the Hare

Once upon a time, there was a hare named Harold. Harold was very fast, and he made sure that all the other forest creatures knew it. He had lots of fun running past skunks and leaping over squirrels. But most of all, Harold loved to race.

"I'm the fastest animal in the whole forest," Harold told a group of critters. "I'm even faster than the wind! Not one of you could beat me in a race."

The other animals were tired of hearing Harold brag, but they were all too polite to interrupt him. All except a tortoise named Tom, that is.

"Hogwash!" Tom cried. "You may be fast, but you can certainly be beaten in a race."

Harold laughed. He couldn't believe that one of the slowest animals he'd ever met was saying this!

"Not a single creature has ever beaten me in a race," Harold replied. "But you're welcome to try."

"I accept your challenge," Tom said. "I'll race you."

Harold laughed, and the other creatures started to snicker. It would be a piece of cake for Harold to beat a tortoise!

"We'll race next Saturday," Harold said. "That should give you plenty of time to practice."

Tom spent the next few days getting ready for the race.
He stretched his legs, and jogged around the lily pond. He ate lots of
dandelions and berries to build up his energy.

Meanwhile, Harold was so sure he'd win the race that he didn't
bother to practice. He lay in the sunshine, took lots of naps, and
chatted with his friends.

On the day of the race, the forest critters gathered at the starting line. Even though they didn't really think Tom would win, they were excited to see him try.

"May the best animal win," Tom said kindly.

"Good luck," Harold replied. "You're going to need it!"

"On your marks," said the referee, "get set... GO!"

Harold took off so quickly that a big gust of wind blew Tom around until he was facing backward. The crowd cheered. What an exciting start!

By the time Tom was facing the right direction, Harold was long gone. Tom set off down the path at a slow and steady pace. A group of snails cheered excitedly.

"Come on, Tom! You can do it!" the snails yelled.

Tom finally reached the first bend in the path. Harold was nowhere to be seen, but Tom wasn't worried. He put one foot in front of the other and continued down the racetrack.

10

Far down the path, Harold was running so fast that the petals blew off the flowers he passed.

I can't believe that silly tortoise thought he could beat me, Harold thought smugly. *I'm definitely going to win this race!*

Harold suddenly skidded to a stop. His friend George was lying under a shady tree, so Harold stopped to chat.

"Hello, Harold," George said. "Why are you in such a hurry?"

"Oh, I'm just running a race," Harold replied. "But it won't be too hard to win, since I'm racing Tom."

As Harold and George laughed at the idea of a tortoise racing a hare, Tom crept past them quietly. The silly hares were so busy chatting that they didn't even notice him!

Just as Tom thought he was safely past them, Harold laughed.

"Look at that tortoise go!" Harold said to George. "He really thinks he's going to beat me."

"Go get him, Harold!" George said.

Harold rushed past Tom, and the tortoise was blown over. When he looked up, he saw Harold disappearing down the path. That pesky hare had passed him again!

Tom stood up and dusted himself off. He took a step, and then another, and continued on his way.

Harold was having lots of fun racing Tom. The tortoise was far behind him, and Harold was certain he would win. Harold did a somersault, and then a cartwheel. He sure liked to show off!

Up ahead, a crowd of animals was waiting at the finish line.

As Harold neared the finish line, he heard the animals cheering. He slowed down to a trot.

What's the hurry? Harold thought to himself. *That tortoise is so far behind, he'll never catch up!*

Sure that he would win, Harold decided to stop and rest for a while. He hopped off the path and into the meadow beside it.

I'll just take a quick nap, he thought to himself. *There's plenty of time to relax!*

With that, Harold laid down in the soft green grass, and fell asleep.

When Tom finally reached the sleeping hare, he wondered why Harold was napping. That's no way to win a race! Tom tiptoed past him very carefully and very quietly. Harold snorted, but he didn't wake up.

The crowd at the finish line started yelling and clapping when they saw Tom. Even though some of them had doubted him, it looked like the tortoise was going to win the race!

"Tom, Tom, he's our man! If he can't do it, no one can!" the crowd cheered.

The crowd cheered so loudly that thcy woke up Harold. He looked around, and was surprised to see Tom nearing the finish line. The hare laughed to himself as he hopped to his feet. That silly tortoise still thought he'd win the race!

Harold sped off down the track, sure that he would catch up to Tom. But he had an awfully long way to go...

Harold suddenly felt very worried. He really shouldn't have stopped to chat with George, or to nap. What a waste of time!

"Come on, Tom!" the crowd cheered. "You're almost there!"

Tom stretched out his long neck, and poked his head over the finish line just as Harold caught up to him. Tom had won the race!

"That was a great race," Tom said to the hare. "No hard feelings?"

"You beat me fair and square," Harold admitted. "I may be fast, but I'm not always very wise. Slow and steady beats hurried and careless!"

From that day forward, Harold worked hard at everything he did. The tortoise and the hare became great friends, and lived happily ever after.